# Welcome to MORNINGTOWN

Blake Liliane Hellman

illustrated by Steven Henry

BLOOMSBURY
CHILDREN'S BOOKS
NEW YORK LONDON OXFORD NEW DELHI SYDNEY

BLOOMSBURY CHILDREN'S BOOKS
Bloomsbury Publishing Inc., part of Bloomsbury Publishing Plc
1385 Broadway, New York, NY 10018

BLOOMSBURY, BLOOMSBURY CHILDREN'S BOOKS, and the Diana logo are trademarks of Bloomsbury Publishing Plc

First published in the United States of America in June 2019
by Bloomsbury Children's Books

Bloomsbury books may be purchased for business or promotional use. For information on bulk
purchases please contact Macmillan Corporate and Premium Sales Department at
specialmarkets@macmillan.com

Library of Congress Cataloging-in-Publication Data
Names: Hellman, Blake Liliane, author. | Henry, Steven, illustrator.
Title: Welcome to Morningtown / by Blake Liliane Hellman ; illustrated by Steven Henry.
Description: New York : Bloomsbury, 2019.
Summary: In Morningtown, animal families of all shapes and sizes are waking up,
getting out of bed, washing up, eating breakfast, and looking forward to a new day.
Identifiers: LCCN 2018045216 (print)  •  LCCN 2018051307 (e-book)
ISBN 978-1-68119-873-6 (hardcover)  •  ISBN 978-1-68119-874-3 (e-book)  •  ISBN 978-1-68119-875-0 (e-PDF)
Subjects: | CYAC: Morning—Fiction. | Animals—Fiction.
Classification: LCC PZ7.1.H4468 We 2019 (print) | LCC PZ7.1.H4468 (e-book) | DDC [E]—dc23
LC record available at https://lccn.loc.gov/2018045216

Art created with pencil, watercolor, and gouache
Typeset in Century Schoolbook
Book design by Jeanette Levy
Printed in China by Leo Paper Products, Heshan, Guangdong
2 4 6 8 10 9 7 5 3 1

To find out more about our authors and books visit www.bloomsbury.com and sign up for our newsletters.

For teacher and guide, Ariel G.,
who's shown me magical places —B. L. H.

For Lucian —S. H.

I<sub>n</sub> Morningtown,
*everyone* is waking.

Stretching . . .

Yawning.

Hopping,

flopping,

splashing awake.

Leaving fluffy beds,

hard beds,

secret beds,

and very special beds.

Down in the deep,
cold dark.

And high in a cozy,
lofty spot.

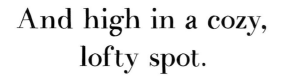

Brushing,

Early birds are
up and at 'em.

flushing,

washing.

It's time to pick out socks and underwear!

Then when you're dressed,
breakfast is next!

Some crunch,

some nibble,

some sip their morning feast.

Hooray, for a
shiny new day!

Full of lessons to learn,

friends to make,

and maybe a
chore or two.

Every day's a surprise, and as the sun rises . . .

busy bees
buzz,

fun bunnies bounce,

and eager beavers
slide into the day.

Welcome to Morningtown!
Everyone is up . . .

. . . except one.